Disney PRINCESS

5 Minute Treasury

PaRragon

Bath · New York · Cologne · Melbourne · Delhi
Hong Kong · Shenzhen · Singapore

This edition published by Parragon Books Ltd in 2016

Parragon Books Ltd
Chartist House
15–17 Trim Street
Bath BA1 1HA, UK
www.parragon.com

ISBN 978-1-4748-4604-2

Printed in China

Contents

Cinderella
The Lost Mice

One clear winter night, the Prince led Cinderella out to the balcony.

"I have a surprise for you," he said, handing her a box.

Inside was a beautiful new coat.

"Oh, it's simply lovely!" Cinderella exclaimed. "Thank you."

It was a pretty and thoughtful gift. The coat would keep her warm during the cold weather.

The next morning, the princess showed her coat to Suzy, one of her mouse friends.

"Isn't the Prince thoughtful?" Cinderella remarked.

"Nice-a! Nice-a!" Suzy exclaimed. The coat sleeve felt warm and cosy – especially compared to where the mice lived.

A few minutes later, Jaq and Gus went into Cinderella's room.
It had been a chilly night in the attic, and the mice were still shivering.

"Cinderelly! Cinderelly!" Jaq called. He knew that if he told the
princess how cold the attic was, she would do something about it.

But Cinderella was rushing off to get dressed for a tea party, so she
didn't hear her friend.

Jaq sighed. It was too cold for the mice to stay in the attic much longer. Cinderella had always been very kind to the mice, and Jaq was sure she would want them to be warm.

So he and Gus called the rest of the mice down from the attic. They sat in front of a blazing fire in Cinderella's room. Before long, their cold paws and tails had warmed up, and their teeth stopped chattering. They'd wait there until Cinderella got back.

Soon, the new housekeeper came in to clean the room.
When she saw the mice, she shrieked and shooed them away.

"Mice don't belong in the castle!" she yelled. "Now get out!"

The housekeeper didn't know that the mice were Cinderella's
friends. She chased them with a broom. The frightened mice
had no choice but to scramble back up to the cold attic.

"Brrrr." Gus began to shiver as soon as the mice were safely upstairs.

The mice really needed the princess's help! But how would they be able to speak to Cinderella when they were afraid to set foot downstairs?

WHAM! Suddenly, the castle gardener barged through the attic door. Before the mice knew what was happening, he had trapped them.

"Now take them outside!" they heard the housekeeper say. "Take them far away so they never return."

Meanwhile, Cinderella's tea party had ended and she and the Prince were out riding. As they rode through the countryside, they saw the castle gardener tending to something in one of the fields.

"Hello," the Prince called out. "It's much too cold to be working outside."

But the gardener did not answer.

The Prince called to him again and still got no reply.

As they rode on, the Prince turned to Cinderella.

"That was odd," he said. "I can't believe he did not hear me. Why wouldn't he answer?"

"Perhaps he was lost in thought?" Cinderella suggested.

Cinderella was right – the gardener had been lost in thought.
He was about to let the mice go as the housekeeper had ordered,
but he was worried about them. He knew it was too cold outside.

Finally, he decided to take the mice to the stables.

"Now don't tell the housekeeper," he told the stable workers.
"But these poor mice need a warm place to stay and a bite to eat."

The mice were very grateful to their new friends.

The mice nestled together in the barn. But as night approached,
the stables got colder. Luckily, the horses were very friendly.
They told the mice to snuggle in their manes to keep warm.

"Thassa nice-a," said Gus as he drifted off to sleep.

Later that night, back at the castle, Cinderella was starting to worry. She hadn't seen the mice since that morning. Jaq and Gus nearly always came by in the evening.

Cinderella was searching for the mice when she ran into the Prince. "Hello!" the Prince said. "Are you looking for the same person I am?"

"No, I don't think so," Cinderella replied. "I'm looking for the mice!"

"Ah," said the Prince. "Well, I am looking for our new housekeeper. Apparently she threw the mice out of the castle today!"

"Oh, no!" Cinderella cried. "Poor dears. They'll freeze outside!"

"Don't worry," the Prince said. "The mice have found a new friend."

He told Cinderella about what the gardener had done.

Together, Cinderella and the Prince went to the stables. They thanked the gardener and the stable workers. Then they gently woke the mice.

"Cinderelly! Cinderelly!" the mice shouted happily.

Cinderella was relieved to see her friends safe and sound. Though the stables had been nice, the mice were glad to return to the castle.

From then on, Cinderella made sure the mice always had a warm place of their own – in one of the main rooms of the castle.

A few nights later, Cinderella and the Prince threw a grand ball. The gardener was the guest of honour. By then, the housekeeper had been properly introduced to the mice, and all was well.

As the guests twirled around the dance floor, the mice celebrated with a banquet of their own, warm and cosy at last.

Ariel and the Whale Song

"Aaaaariel!" called a voice from beneath the brilliant blue water.

Ariel dived into the sea and found her friend Flounder waiting for her.

"We should find Sebastian," Ariel said. "I promised him I would sing at the concert today."

Sebastian had organized a special concert for the first day of summer. Ariel was sure he'd be setting up for it already. She was also sure that he would not be happy if she was late.

Ariel and Flounder swam side by side towards home. Ariel admired the beautiful coral reef as they passed it.

There are always new things to discover in the ocean, she thought.
I wonder if I have time to stop off at the shipwreck before –

"Ah!" came a shout from behind her. Flounder was quivering and
covering his eyes with his fins.

"Oh, Flounder, it's just a little crab," Ariel assured him. She swam over
to her frightened friend. "Really, there's nothing to be afraid of!"

She peeled Flounder's fins away from his eyes as the crab scuttled away.
Flounder breathed a sigh of relief.

"We need to toughen you up a bit." Ariel smiled. She loved her friend,
but even she knew he was a bit of a scaredy-fish.

When Ariel and Flounder found Sebastian, he was leading the orchestra very quickly through the final song of the concert.

"Sebastian," Ariel said, "slow down. We have plenty of time to get ready."

"But Princess, we don't," Sebastian told her. "This isn't just a concert to celebrate the start of summer. We are performing for the whales!"

"The whales?" Ariel asked.

"Yes. Don't you know? The whales are migrating through Coral Cove today. All of them! And I promised your father this concert would be timed exactly to them passing over us."

Sebastian continued, but Ariel stopped listening. The whales? She would love to meet a whale! But how could she if she was singing at the concert?

"And if this concert isn't perfect," Sebastian was saying, "Ariel ... Ariel?"

Ariel snapped out of her thoughts. "The concert will be perfect!" she assured him as she started to swim away.

"Where are you going?" Sebastian cried.

"I just need to get something from my treasure grotto," Ariel said, thinking quickly. "I promise I'll be back before the concert!"

And then she swam off with Flounder following close behind.

"All right, Flounder. Are you up for a quick
trip to Coral Cove?" Ariel asked with a sly smile.

"Coral Cove? But ... but why are you going there?"
Flounder asked.

"To meet the whales," she told him. "They never visit us
at the palace, so this is my only chance."

Soon they reached the edge of the reef, where Coral Cove began.
Even Ariel felt a little nervous entering unchartered waters. And was
it just her, or had it actually got colder?

"I – I don't see any whales here," Flounder stammered.

"Me neither ..." Ariel added, slightly disappointed.

She looked around, hoping for some sort of sign. And just then,
she heard one.

Ariel listened carefully. The noise seemed to be coming from above. The closer she listened, the more it sounded like a song.

"Flounder, follow me!" Ariel said excitedly. She swam quickly towards the brilliant blue light that broke through the ocean's surface. The tune was getting louder.

Ariel swam all the way up to the water's surface, hoping to find whatever was making the beautiful song. But as she looked around, she saw nothing but the wide, flat ocean. She frowned, disappointed.

"Oh, Flounder. There's nothing here," said Ariel. "And we need to get back for the concert soon or Sebastian will be upset with us. Flounder?"

Ariel looked around. Where had her friend gone? She was about to dive back under when Flounder suddenly burst into the air!

"It was – it was a shark!" Flounder cried. "A shark!"

Ariel tried to calm her friend.

"Flounder, sharks don't come into these waters near Coral Cove, remember? It's too close to land for them," Ariel told him.

Then she gasped. Something was approaching them and it sure looked like a shark. Ariel dived beneath the waves to get a better look.

The shape came closer ... and closer ... until it was so close that Ariel could make out a giant tail. But before she could work out who the tail belonged to, it made a giant swooping motion and an underwater wave surrounded Ariel and Flounder with bubbles.

When the bubbles cleared, Ariel was amazed at what she saw.

It was a mummy whale and her baby. And they were singing!

"Whale song," Ariel whispered.

"It's beautiful," Flounder said, amazed – and also relieved.

Ariel and Flounder floated next to the whales for a few moments, knowing they might never get this close again. Ariel listened carefully to the melody. Then she sang back to them. The whales smiled at her and continued to sing the tune, and Ariel joined in.

Suddenly, the two whales headed straight towards the ocean's surface and flew into the air. They created a beautiful arc over the water and then belly-flopped on to the smooth surface of the sea.

The huge waves sent Ariel and Flounder soaring into the air. When they landed back in the water, they both had to catch their breath. Then they burst into laughter.

"That was pretty fun!" Flounder cried, still giggling.
"Thanks for making me come along, Ariel."

Ariel smiled. It had been an amazing afternoon.

But now it was time to get back to Sebastian.

Ariel and Flounder arrived just in time for the concert.

When it was time for Ariel's solo, she decided to sing the beautiful whale song she had learned from the mummy and baby whale.

As she continued to sing, she could feel the water's currents change and she knew the whales were passing by. She smiled and sang even louder to celebrate the start of summer and to honour her new friends.

Disney
PRINCESS

Beauty and the Beast

Belle and the Castle Puppy

Belle was strolling through the castle garden one chilly spring day when she heard a whimpering sound. A puppy was huddled outside the castle gates. He looked cold and dirty.

"Oh, you poor thing!" Belle cried. "Let's get you warmed up and fed." She wrapped the puppy in her red cloak and hurried to the castle.

Belle and the enchanted objects gave the puppy a bath. The coat stand brought a towel.

When he was clean and dry, the puppy ate a bowl of warm stew.

"He's so cute! I hope we can keep him!" Chip the teacup exclaimed.

All the enchanted objects were happy to have a guest. But the foot stool remembered when he had been a real dog, just like the puppy. What if Belle and the Beast liked this dog better? The foot stool tried to get Belle's attention. With a funny little *grrr*, he raced around the kitchen. But no one noticed.

A moment later, the puppy barked at the door.

"Do you want to go out to play?" Belle asked.

As Belle and the others followed the puppy outside, they didn't see the foot stool slink out behind them and walk in a different direction. They laughed as Belle threw sticks for the puppy to fetch.

The Beast walked up to Belle a while later.

"Someone has dug up my roses!" he exclaimed.

Then the Beast saw the puppy.

"Did that dog ruin my garden? Get rid of him –
NOW!" the Beast roared as he stomped away.

A moment later, the foot stool ran past Belle and the others. His legs were muddy.

"The foot stool dug up the garden!" Belle exclaimed.

"But why?" asked Lumiere the candelabrum.

As Belle watched the foot stool chase after the Beast, she suddenly understood.

"Oh, poor little guy," she said. "He just wanted some attention, too!"

Suddenly, the puppy raced after the foot stool, barking playfully. They both disappeared among the trees.

"What if they don't catch up with the Beast? They'll get lost!" Belle exclaimed. "I have to bring them back safely."

"But it's getting dark," Mrs Potts protested.

Belle looked at the long shadows creeping through the forest. Clutching her cloak tightly, she took a deep breath and headed for the trees.

"Wait!" Lumiere called to Belle. "I'll come and light your way."

"Thank you," Belle said as she picked up the candelabrum. "I'm glad you're coming."

"Me, too. I think," Lumiere replied. But his flames flickered nervously.

Belle walked along a path. She had come this way before.

"Puppy! Foot stool!" she called.

She hoped that they had met up with the Beast. She was looking forward to returning to the castle.

A moment later, something rustled in the bushes.

"What is that?" Lumiere whispered.

"I hope it's just squirrels," Belle answered.

"They must be very big squirrels," Lumiere replied.

Belle picked up a large stick. Then she
and Lumiere walked on, calling for the
puppy and the foot stool.

Belle realized that the puppy and foot stool had got lost. She was determined to find them.

A short while later, Belle heard loud barking.

"I think we've found them!" Lumiere exclaimed.

Belle followed the sound until she came into a clearing. The foot stool and puppy stood under an enormous tree. The puppy was growling and barking loudly.

"What's wrong?" Belle wondered aloud. Then she looked round and gasped. Two large wolves were nearby.

"The puppy is protecting the foot stool!" Lumiere exclaimed.

"He's too small to stop those wolves for long," Belle said. "He needs help!"

Quickly, Belle put Lumiere on the ground and lit the stick she had been carrying. She ran towards the wolves, swinging the stick.

"Get away! Get away!" she shouted.

But the wolves didn't move.

Just then, the Beast showed up. The wolves ran away, yelping with fear.

"The puppy tried to save the foot stool!" Belle told the Beast.

"They are brave little fellows," the Beast answered.

Cradling the puppy in one arm and the foot stool in the other, he led Belle back to the castle.

Later that night, everyone settled by the fireplace. Belle watched the Beast stroke the foot stool and feed biscuits to the puppy.

"May the puppy stay until I can find him a home?" she asked.

The Beast cleared his throat.

"His home is here – with us," he answered gruffly.

Belle smiled. She was glad that the Beast had changed his mind.

The very next day, the Beast presented the puppy and the foot stool with shiny badges. From now on, they would be the official protectors of the castle.

Yip! Yip! Woof! Woof! They couldn't have been more excited.

THE PRINCESS AND THE FROG

A Surprise Guest

It was a balmy afternoon in New Orleans – perfect for a night with friends.

"Charlotte, honey!" Big Daddy LaBouff called to his daughter. "How about going to Tiana's Palace for supper tonight?"

"Oh, Daddy, that would be wonderful! Just give me a minute to change."

A little later, Big Daddy and Charlotte drove off. But they didn't realize their dog, Stella, was asleep in the back of the car!

When the LaBouffs arrived at the restaurant, a jazz band was on stage. Louis the alligator was playing his trumpet.

"Charlotte! How are you?" Princess Tiana exclaimed. She was happy to see her best friend. "Big Daddy, would you like to sit with my mama and Naveen's parents?"

"Why, I can't think of anyone better to share my supper with than Eudora and your in-laws," he replied.

Soon Tiana's family and friends were settled at a big table. The princess walked around the dining room to make sure her other guests were happy, too.

Meanwhile, Stella had woken up. The dog climbed out of the LaBouffs' car and looked around. Immediately, she caught the mouthwatering scent of Tiana's beignets. Stella followed her nose right into the restaurant kitchen.

"*Lookee* here!" shouted one of the cooks. "We have a visitor! Here you go, puppy – have some of this gumbo. It's a new recipe."

Stella eagerly tasted the dish. It was delicious! A moment later, a waiter threw her a large bone. The dog couldn't believe her good luck.

Stella spent the whole evening in the kitchen. While Charlotte and Big Daddy dined to Louis' jazz music and talked with their friends, Stella was getting all kinds of treats.

Late that night, after the last jazz song had been played, all of the guests went home. Charlotte and Big Daddy hadn't realized that Stella was also at the restaurant! "Ta-ta!" Charlotte called as they left.

Eudora left with Naveen's parents. Turning to her daughter, she said, "I have never heard the band play quite that well. And that new gumbo – absolutely delicious. I'll see you tomorrow, sweetheart."

After Princess Tiana walked her family to the door, she went back to the dining room to finish cleaning up.

A few minutes later, Louis and the band went to the kitchen for their evening meal.

As they walked in, Stella began to bark. *Grrr! Woof!* She was terrified of the giant alligator.

"Oh, now hold on, little dog!" Louis said to Stella. "I'm not here to eat you. I just wanted a taste of the chef's new gumbo!"

But Stella was frightened. She kept barking.
The kitchen staff and the band members looked
at each other. They weren't sure what to do.

In the dining room, Tiana and Naveen heard the barking. They rushed to see what was causing the commotion.

Tiana recognized the LaBouffs' pet at once. "Stella? What are you doing here?" she asked. "Don't worry. Louis is our friend. He wouldn't hurt anybody."

"That's true!" Naveen cried, putting his arm round Louis. "He is nothing but a big guy with an even bigger heart."

The alligator peeked out from behind his tail. He didn't understand why the dog was so upset.

Stella looked at him suspiciously.

"Go ahead," Princess Tiana encouraged the dog. "Just go over and make friends."

Cautiously, Stella walked towards Louis. The alligator stayed very still. He didn't want to frighten the dog all over again.

"See? Nothing to be scared about!" Naveen said.

Soon Stella realized Louis was harmless. The dog wagged her tail. Then she smelled some delicious chicken.

Tiana smiled. "Let's get dinner for you all."

The princess and the kitchen staff quickly put together a supper out of that evening's leftovers.

Everyone went into the dining room. The staff ate while Prince Naveen played the ukulele. Louis picked up his trumpet and joined in the song. A few of the waiters and waitresses began to dance. Stella didn't pay much attention, though. She was eating some of Tiana's beignets.

A while later, the staff headed home. Tomorrow would be another busy day at Tiana's Palace.

"Come along, Stella," Tiana told the dog. "Time for you to go, too."

The prince and princess took Stella to Charlotte's house. No one had noticed she was missing yet!

"Goodnight, Stella," Princess Tiana said, giving the dog a big hug. "Now that you know how much fun we have at the restaurant, you should come by more often."

Woof! Woof! Stella barked. She hadn't expected to have such an adventure that night. She knew she'd return to Tiana's Palace the next chance she got.

Beauty and the Beast

Belle's Friendship Invention

"Oh, Papa, isn't it exciting?" Belle asked. She and her father, Maurice, were walking towards the centre of town. It was the day of the first annual Invention Convention. Maurice had been organizing it for months. And the big day had finally arrived!

"It certainly is," said Maurice. "People from all over the countryside are coming. I have a feeling there are some big surprises in store."

When Belle and her father arrived, the town square was bustling with more activity than ever before! Townsfolk were eagerly setting up booths to present their incredible inventions.

"Why don't you go and explore while I get ready?" Maurice said.

Belle could hardly wait. She loved seeing new inventions and there were so many on display.

Everywhere Belle looked there was a new, imaginative contraption.
Some had lots of bells and whistles. Others were quite practical.
Some were simple and sweet.

Just when Belle thought she'd seen it all, she spied a crowd
gathering across the square. Belle squeezed through the thick circle
of people to see what everyone was 'oohing' and 'ahhing' over.

There must be something extra exciting over here, Belle thought.

When she reached the centre of the crowd, Belle was amazed
by what she saw. In the middle of the circle was an invention
unlike any of the others – and the inventor was a girl Belle's age!

The girl was just about to demonstrate how her machine
worked, and she was looking for a volunteer.

"What's your name?" the girl asked Belle.

"I'm Belle."

"My name is Simone. Would you like to be my volunteer?" Simone guided Belle over to her invention. "Please place these leaves on the screen."

Belle did as she was asked. Then Simone closed the flap on the machine and pushed a button. The leaves were pushed through the machine and came out as sheets of writing paper!

As the people left, Belle helped Simone collect her pile of leaf paper. "How did you think of such a clever invention?" Belle asked.

"When I was little, I always wanted to build an invention that could spread happiness," Simone explained. "One day I realized that special notes make people happy. Sometimes you even make a new friend with a note. So I decided to invent a machine to create paper as special as the notes."

Belle looked at the stack of beautiful leaf paper. "That gives me a fantastic idea!" she said.

Simone look down at the paper, confused.

"Why don't we write some nice messages on these pieces of paper and deliver them to the people in town?" Belle suggested.

"How wonderful!" cried Simone.

But who would they write to first?

Just then, the fresh scent of nearby flowers caught their attention, so the girls wrote a note to the florist:

Thank you for selling beautiful flowers.

Belle and Simone delivered the note, but they didn't sign it. They wanted to spread happiness in secret. It made it more exciting!

They watched as the florist opened his message. Reading it seemed to make him very happy!

"This is fun!" said Simone. "Let's write another one."

"Who should we write to next?"
asked Simone.

"How about the bookseller?" Belle
suggested. "His books always make me happy.
I think a nice note would be the perfect way to say 'thank you'."
Belle and Simone wrote a note to the bookseller and delivered it in secret!

The bookseller was with a customer when he discovered the note.
Belle and Simone watched as he opened it, read it and smiled.

Belle winked. "Your invention is working!" she whispered to Simone.
"It really is spreading happiness!"

Together, the girls delivered nice messages to many of the townsfolk.
Soon they had only one sheet of Simone's paper left.

"Who should we write our last note to?" Simone asked.

"I know just the person," said Belle.

A short while later, Belle and Simone delivered a very special handwritten message to Maurice. This time, they didn't hide.

Dear Papa, thank you for organizing this wonderful convention. It brought two new friends together.
– Belle and Simone

Maurice chuckled. "You're quite welcome." Then he handed the girls a new book each. "The bookseller asked me to give these to you. He recognized your handwriting and wanted to thank you. The note made him very happy."

At the end of the day, the convention was over. It was time for Simone to pack up her invention and say goodbye.

"I had a wonderful time," Simone told Belle. "I'm so glad we met. And I wanted to give you this." She handed Belle a beautiful fresh stack of leaf paper. "Promise you'll write?"

Belle hugged Simone. "Of course," she said. "And you must write back to me. I want to hear about all the incredible new inventions you come up with!"

Belle waved as Simone's cart rolled away. She was going to miss her new friend.

Later that night, when Belle opened her new book, she was surprised to find a special note from Simone tucked inside.

And when she read it, she knew their friendship would last.

Belle couldn't wait to see Simone again – she was sure their next adventure would be even more fun.

Snow White and the Three Giants

S now White visited her friends, the Dwarfs, very often and she knew the path to their cottage well.

But one beautiful spring day, because Snow White was busy talking with the woodland creatures and admiring the lovely flowers, she took a wrong turn by mistake.

Snow White was singing a cheerful song
in the sunshine and didn't notice the
strange path she had wandered down.
Soon, she arrived at a cottage in
a clearing. She waved goodbye to her
friends and skipped towards the door.

Snow White was so excited
to see the Dwarfs that she didn't
notice the door was unusually heavy.
But once she stepped inside, Snow White
soon realized this wasn't the Dwarfs' cottage.
"Oh my!" she exclaimed.

Instead of a neat row of seven little chairs, she saw three enormous chairs.

Instead of the cosy kitchen she knew so well, a fire roared and crackled in an enormous hearth.

Snow White was amazed at how large the cottage was, as she gazed up at the gigantic dining table.

Suddenly, the ground began to shake.

"Oh no!" Snow White gasped.

With a groan, the huge door opened and in came three of the tallest people Snow White had ever seen. The three giants stepped into the cottage and lumbered towards her.

At first Snow White was a little frightened – she had heard a lot of stories about giants. But the giants were laughing and joking merrily as their loud voices boomed around the cottage. The sound of their laughter gave Snow White courage.

How scary could these giants be? Snow White thought.

Snow White cleared her throat and stepped into view.

"Excuse me," she said.

The giants jumped back in surprise at the little voice below them.

"I'm sorry," Snow White continued. "I let myself in by mistake."

"Oh!" said the largest giant. "You scared us. We don't get visitors often."

Snow White laughed. She couldn't understand how she could have scared the giants ... they were so much bigger than her!

The giants looked down at the little stranger in their cottage and smiled. "But now you're here," said one of them, "you should join us for dinner." He helped Snow White climb onto a chair, but it was too big for her.

"You'll need some cushions," he said and helped Snow White reach the huge dining table.

The giants were very kind hosts and made Snow White comfortable. They all laughed together as they realized that Snow White was too small to lift their giant cutlery. The middle-sized giant found a small plate and glass for Snow White to use.

"Thank you," said Snow White. "You're all so kind!"

Snow White enjoyed a wonderful meal with the giants and made three new, very large friends.

The next day, Snow White told the Dwarfs about her adventures in the woods with the giants.

"G-g-giants?" stammered Bashful.

Sleepy yawned. "Aren't they dangerous?"

"Not at all," Snow White said.

Snow White told the Dwarfs how friendly and welcoming the giants had been to her.

"Don't trust them!" Grumpy interrupted. "You can't trust anyone that tall."
Snow white smiled at her friend. "But I'm taller than you," she said.
Grumpy crossed his arms and frowned, he wasn't convinced.
"Well, you'll just have to meet them," Snow White said.

Back at the castle, Snow White thought about what Grumpy had said.

She knew the Dwarfs and giants would all be great friends if they were given the chance. So, she decided to have a party to introduce the giants to the Dwarfs.

On the day of the party, the Dwarfs and giants arrived at
the castle. There was one enormous table with three huge chairs
and one small table with seven little chairs.

Once her friends were all seated, Snow White announced her
party game. "We're going to play snap. I'll point out something
about me and if it's true for you, shout 'Snap!' – and then it's
someone else's turn."

The Dwarfs and giants sat patiently, waiting for
Snow White to begin the game.

Snow White stood in front of the Dwarfs and
her new friends the giants.

"I have two eyes," she said.

"Snap!" yelled the Dwarfs.

"Snap!" yelled the giants.

Confused for a moment, the Dwarfs and the giants looked around at each other and nodded. They all had two eyes, just like Snow White.

Snow White turned to Bashful, it was his turn next.

Bashful slowly stood up from his stool and politely took off his hat. Bashful was especially shy in front of the giants, but he wanted to play the game for his friend Snow White.

"Um, I have two ears," he stammered.

"Snap!" called the Dwarfs.

"Snap!" called the giants.

The Dwarfs and the giants waggled their ears at each other and laughed. Snow White smiled as she noticed that even Grumpy was starting to join in the game.

Now it was the largest giant's turn. He thought for a moment and soon realized the answer was right in front of his face.

"Ahem, I have one nose" he said, pointing with his very large finger at his very big nose.

"Snap!" shouted the Dwarfs.

"Snap!" shouted the giants.

The Dwarfs and giants all stood up with their fingers on their noses and laughed.

Although the giants were very big and the Dwarfs were very small, they each had two eyes, two ears and one nose.

"I guess we have a lot in common after all," Grumpy muttered.

"Yes, you do!" said Snow White. "And there's one more thing you have in common – you are all my friends!"

Grumpy shook hands with one of the giants.

Perhaps tall people aren't so very different after all, he thought.

Everybody spent the rest of the afternoon enjoying the party. The Dwarfs and giants were happy discovering all the other things they had in common, and the exciting things that were different.

Snow White smiled to herself. She was glad she had taken a different path through the woods that day.

THE PRINCESS AND THE FROG
Tiana's Friendship Fix-up

Charlotte rummaged through her wardrobe. She was looking for the perfect dress to wear to dinner that night, but she didn't like anything she tried on.

"I've got nothing new to wear, Tia. We need to go shopping."

Tiana groaned. "I hardly have time to sit, let alone shop, Lottie."

Charlotte pouted. "Oh, you're always so busy with your restaurant and Naveen. We need a friendship fix-up, Tia. I just want to spend time with you."

Charlotte had a point. Tiana had been very busy.

"All right," she said. "We can go!"

Charlotte led Tiana to the Bayou Boutique and held up a pink dress.

"Isn't this darling?" she said.

"That's swell, Lottie," Tiana replied. "Shall we get it and go?"

But Charlotte wasn't so sure. She tried on dress after dress after dress.

Hours later, Charlotte finally started picking which dresses she wanted.

"Almost done?" Tiana asked hopefully.

"Just one more thing," Charlotte replied, grabbing a dress from her growing pile. "This dress is perfect for you!"

"Me?" Tiana said. "But I love the dresses Mama made for me. I don't need another."

"And I love them, too," Charlotte said. "But there's always room for something new!"

"I don't know, Lottie...." said Tiana.

Charlotte tried and tried to convince Tiana to get the dress, but Tiana refused. Charlotte could tell her friend was starting to get frustrated. This shopping trip wasn't going at all like Charlotte had hoped!

"All right," Charlotte said, dropping the dress. "If you don't want to shop, let's do something else instead." Charlotte thought for a moment, then snapped her fingers. "I know just the thing!"

Charlotte led Tiana to the kitchen of Tiana's restaurant.

"I can help you cook!" Charlotte said. "Won't that be fun?"

Tiana wasn't so sure, but she thought she should at least give it a try.
Together, Tiana and Charlotte started making the dough for Tiana's
signature dish – beignets!

Their first batch of beignets was a smashing success. But then Tiana was called away to talk to a customer in the dining room.

"Can you handle the next batch on your own?" Tiana asked.

"No problem, Tia!" Charlotte said. "You can count on me."

After Tiana left, Charlotte rolled out the dough.

These beignets need some pizzazz, Charlotte thought, and she cut each beignet into one of her favourite shapes.

Charlotte placed the beignets into the fryer to cook, then she started on another batch of dough. She hoped Tiana would be back soon – cooking wasn't nearly as much fun without her best friend.

Charlotte was about to go looking for Tiana when she caught a whiff of something that made her heart skip a beat.

Smoke was pouring out of Charlotte's frying pot – she had left the beignets cooking for too long!

Tiana ran in from the dining room. "Lottie! What did you do?"

Charlotte felt terrible for ruining the beignets. This wasn't what she wanted to happen. She started to cry and ran from the kitchen.

Charlotte didn't stop running until she got home.
The day had been a complete disaster. She just hoped
that Tiana would forgive her.

Tiana wished that she could go after Charlotte, but there was a kitchen to clean and meals to cook for hungry customers.

She got straight to work throwing out the burned beignets, but then she saw one of the special shaped beignets that Charlotte had made. Tiana's heart sank. She hoped her best friend was okay.

Later that night, both Charlotte and Tiana knew they had
to find each other. Charlotte headed over to Main Street,
hoping to run into Tiana. Tiana did the same.

In no time, the friends spotted each other. Tiana ran to
Charlotte and hugged her tightly.

"I'm sorry!" Charlotte cried. "My friendship fix-up was
a complete disaster."

"I'm sorry, too," Tiana said. "You were just trying to find
something fun for us to do together."

"I want to spend time with you, Tia, but maybe shopping or cooking isn't the right thing for us," Charlotte said.

"I agree," Tiana said. "So what can we do?"

Tiana looked up as if to find an answer – and she did! "Look, Lottie!"

"*The Frog Prince*," Charlotte said.

"Our favourite!" they said together.

After the show, Tiana said, "That was amazing."

"Oh, yes!" Charlotte smiled. "But the way your mama told the story when we were girls is still the best."

"Thank you, Lottie," Tiana said, giving Charlotte another hug. "This was the perfect friendship fix-up!"

Tangled

Rapunzel Finds a Friend

Long before Rapunzel knew she was a princess and before she left her tower for an adventure across the kingdom, she was a lonely little girl. Her tower was very tall and hidden deep within the forest, far away from the rest of the kingdom.

Mother Gothel would often leave Rapunzel alone in the tower for days on end. Rapunzel would stare out of the window and wonder about the adventures that awaited her in the world beyond the tower.

More than anything, she wanted some company – a friend she could share adventures with. But the tower was so tall that Rapunzel could only gaze longingly at the animals playing together in the forest below.

The only creatures that could reach the great heights of the tower were butterflies, bees and the occasional bird. Rapunzel longed to make friends with the flying creatures.

But butterflies are notoriously skittish and would flitter away as Rapunzel reached out her little hands. Bees do not like hugs – they buzzed off to enjoy the flowers in the forest.

Rapunzel would share seeds with the birds, but they never stayed around very long. She watched as they soared away into the distance. She wished she could join them on their journey.

Since friends were scarce, Rapunzel decided to fill each day learning an exciting new activity.

First, Rapunzel tried painting, but she was disappointed. Her finished artwork didn't look as good as she had imagined.

Next, Rapunzel tried baking. She hoped that one day she
would be able to share her creations with all her friends.
Sadly her first cake came out burned and black.

Finally Rapunzel tried gardening. If she couldn't go down to
the forest, she would fill the tower with beautiful plants and flowers.
Rapunzel waited and waited, but still her seeds didn't sprout.

Rapunzel was sad. She had tried
all of these activities and couldn't
do any of them.

"Worst day ever," said Rapunzel.
"I can't paint, I can't bake and I
can't grow even one strawberry."

But just as she was about to put away her trowel,
Rapunzel noticed a strange pattern in the dirt.
Looking closer, she realized they were tiny footprints.
"Let's see where else they show up," she said.

A while later, Rapunzel found the same tiny
footprints in her paint. They led all over the floor.

When the prints appeared in her flour, Rapunzel knew something was definitely up.

"This is a mystery," she said. "I love mysteries!"

Rapunzel was excited. She came up with a plan to find out who the footprints belonged to.

From then on, whenever Rapunzel created art, she spilled a little paint. Whenever she baked, she sprinkled a little flour on the table. Whenever she gardened, she sprinkled a little dirt on the floor. Rapunzel wanted to see if the prints would reappear ... and they always did!

Rapunzel spent a lot of time
practising her favourite hobbies.
The more she practised, the better
she became! Soon she was painting beautiful
pictures of her favourite flowers, baking delicious
cakes and growing strong, healthy plants.

One day, as she was picking strawberries by the windowsill, Rapunzel noticed an odd-shaped berry among the others. She reached for the berry and it suddenly changed colour! Standing in front of her was a small, green chameleon frozen with fear.

At first, Rapunzel was a little frightened too, but then she smiled. "So you're the one who's been leaving the little footprints!" she said.

The chameleon nodded shyly.

Rapunzel was delighted! She had solved the mystery of the footprints and found a new creature to be friends with.

Rapunzel didn't have much experience of making friends, but she knew that everything just needed a little practice.

"My name is Rapunzel," said the little girl. "I'll call you Pascal."

The chameleon was encouraged by Rapunzel's smiling face and kind words, but he was still very shy. Rapunzel wondered how she could make the chameleon feel welcome.

"Would you like some cake?" Rapunzel asked.

The chameleon nodded again, this time with more courage.

Finally Rapunzel had a friend she could share her baking creations with!

After that special day, Rapunzel and Pascal became the best of friends. Rapunzel learned that Pascal never said no to cake. And Pascal learned that Rapunzel was the best friend a chameleon could ever ask for.

Rapunzel wasn't lonely anymore and Pascal didn't have to hide –
apart from when they played hide and seek, of course.

Rapunzel never stopped dreaming about the world beyond her tower.
But she knew that she and Pascal would go on an adventure one day.

As friends, they could achieve anything together.

Cinderella

Cinderella's Best-Ever Creations

Cinderella gets invited to many grand events.
But every year, her favourite invitation is to the
harvest dance at the neighbouring village.

This year, Cinderella wanted to do something special for the villagers.

"I know," she said to her mice friends, "there are four little girls in the village. I'm going to make them each a new dress."

"That's a great idea!" squeaked Jaq.

"Those little girls will feel so, so special!" Gus clapped.

So Cinderella set to work creating the first beautiful little dress. First, she laid out the fabric. Next, she cut out the pattern. Then she sewed together all of the pieces.

Tweet, tweet, tweet sang the birds, as they helped Cinderella make the finishing touches to the dress.

Finally, the first dress was done – and it looked beautiful!

Cinderella started work on the other three dresses for the girls.

On the day of the celebration, Cinderella filled the carriage with her four new creations. The mice hopped in, too. As they reached the village, the girls ran out to greet them.

"H-here they come!" squealed Gus.

"But wait, wait!" shouted Jaq. "There are five girls!"

"Oh dear, there must be a new family in the village," said Cinderella. "What are we going to do?"

Cinderella stepped down from her carriage.
"To thank you all for inviting me, I wanted to
surprise you with new dresses," she told the girls.
"But I'm afraid I've only made four."

"What if we all shared a part of our new dresses?" asked one girl. "Then maybe you'd have enough cloth to make our friend a dress, too?"

"I was thinking the same thing!" said Cinderella.

The girls didn't waste a moment. They carried their dresses to a nearby table and laid them down gently.

Snip, snip, snip, snip, went the scissors as Cinderella carefully cut off some ruffles.

Swish, swoosh, rustled the cloth as Gus and the girls gathered it all together.

As Cinderella started creating the new dress, the girls found more ways to share.

"You can use some purple bows from my dress for decoration," said one of the girls.

"Here's some blue fabric
from mine!" added another.

"Here's my yellow fabric!"
said another.

"And here's some of my pink fabric!"
added the fourth girl.

When Cinderella was finished, she gave each of the five
girls their new dress.

"Thank you!" they shouted.

"My thanks to you all," said Cinderella. "With your help,
these dresses have become some of my best-ever creations."

"Let's celebrate!" squeaked Jaq.

"Yup, yup," giggled Gus. "Let's dance."

"This way," said the eldest girl, taking Cinderella by the hand.

Cinderella and the girls joined the other villagers to celebrate
the harvest dance. All the girls looked beautiful in their dresses.
But for Cinderella the most special dress was the fifth one,
because the girls had made it together for their new friend.

Disney PRINCESS

Tangled

Rapunzel's Story

Once upon a time, there was a magical kingdom ruled by a good queen and a kind king. They were happy until the queen became very sick.

The king had heard of a flower with healing powers and sent his guards to dig it up. Unfortunately, the flower belonged to a wicked woman named Mother Gothel.

Losing the flower made Mother Gothel furious. So when the king and queen had a baby, she stole the child away!

Mother Gothel hid the girl, Rapunzel, in a secret tower for almost 18 years. It turned out that Rapunzel's hair, which was magnificently long, had the same healing powers as the flower. Mother Gothel used it to keep herself young and never told the girl she wasn't really her mother.

The queen and king never forgot their lost princess. Each year, on her birthday, they sent lanterns floating through the night sky.

Rapunzel didn't know that the floating lights she saw from her window were lanterns. But her dearest wish was to see the lights up close. "Not just from my window," she said.

But Mother Gothel wouldn't let her go. She needed Rapunzel's magic in order to stay young. Instead, she told Rapunzel that the world outside was a scary place, too dangerous for her.

"Trust me, pet," she said. "Mother knows best."

One day Mother Gothel went away on a trip. Before long, someone climbed the tower. He slipped through the window and – *BANG*! Rapunzel knocked him out with a frying pan.

The man, Flynn Rider, was a thief on the run from the palace guards. Rapunzel searched his bag. Inside was a stolen crown. She tried it on – it felt strangely familiar....

Rapunzel knew this was her only chance to see the floating lights. Flynn could be her guide outside the tower! When Flynn woke up, she offered him a deal.

"Deal?" Flynn asked. He was still dazed from the frying pan.

Rapunzel showed him her paintings of the floating lights.

"Take me to these," she said.

Flynn shook his head. "No can do."

He did not want to go to the city. He was trying to hide from the Stabbington brothers, two thieves he had been in business with. The palace guards were also still chasing him.

But Rapunzel had a bargaining chip – the crown. She'd return it only if Flynn helped her.

So Flynn reluctantly climbed down the tower and Rapunzel used her hair to lower herself to the ground.

The outside world was like a dream come true to her. She'd never run through grass before or climbed a tree, or sat in a field of flowers.

Still, she felt nervous. Mother Gothel had said the outside world was scary. And Mother Gothel wouldn't lie ... would she?

Flynn tried to frighten Rapunzel into going home. He took her to the scariest place he knew – the Snuggly Duckling. It was a tavern full of thugs!

The thugs glared at Rapunzel, but when she sang about her dream of seeing the lanterns, they all became friends. The men even showed Rapunzel and Flynn a secret passage out of the tavern ... just in time, too. The palace guards had tracked down Flynn and his stolen crown.

As they were escaping, Flynn hurt his hand on a sharp rock. That night, Rapunzel wrapped her hair round it, and his hand was healed!

Flynn was amazed, so Rapunzel explained about her magical hair. "But once it's cut," she said, "it loses its power."

They sat close together by the campfire. Flynn was starting to fall for Rapunzel. And Rapunzel liked Flynn a lot, too. But could she trust him?

Meanwhile, Mother Gothel had
discovered that Rapunzel was gone.
She began to search for her.

The next day was Rapunzel's birthday.
Flynn led her to town, which was just as
wonderful as the woods. She and Flynn
danced and ate cake, and then they took
a boat to watch the lanterns.

"For the best day of your life,
I figure you should have
a decent seat," Flynn said.

Twilight came, and glowing lanterns filled the sky.
Rapunzel was so excited to see the lights that she
almost tipped the boat over.

"I have something for you, too," she told Flynn.
She handed him the crown. She finally trusted him.
Flynn knew what he had to do.

Flynn went ashore and tried to give the crown to the Stabbington brothers – but the thieves knocked him out. Then they found Rapunzel and convinced her that Flynn had turned her in.

"A fair trade," they said. "A crown for the girl with the magic hair."

"No!" Rapunzel cried. She tried to run away, but she couldn't.

THUMP! CRASH! Mother Gothel rushed in. She rescued Rapunzel from the thieves. But she didn't tell Rapunzel she'd told the brothers to capture her in the first place.

Mother Gothel and Rapunzel returned to the tower. But Rapunzel couldn't stop thinking of everything she'd seen.

Suddenly, all the pieces fell into place.

"I'm the lost princess," she realized.

Mother Gothel froze.

"It was you!" Rapunzel said bitterly. "I should have been hiding from *you*."

Instantly, Mother Gothel stopped pretending. She tied up Rapunzel.

Soon Flynn came to the tower, looking for Rapunzel, and Mother Gothel hurt him. Rapunzel knew she could heal Flynn with her hair.

"I'll stay with you," she promised Mother Gothel. "Just let me save him."

"Swear it," Mother Gothel said. And Rapunzel did.

But Flynn refused to let Mother Gothel win. Grabbing a shard from a broken mirror, he sliced off Rapunzel's hair. Immediately, it turned brown.

"What have you done?" Mother Gothel shrieked.

As Rapunzel's hair lost its power, Mother Gothel became very old. Only the hair had been keeping her young. Soon, she faded to dust.

Rapunzel held Flynn tight. Without her hair, she couldn't heal him. He slipped away.

A single tear fell from Rapunzel's face. It landed on Flynn and began to glow. His eyes opened. The magic in her tear had saved him!

Overjoyed, Rapunzel and Flynn went to the palace.

Rapunzel was welcomed by the king and queen – her real mother and father. They were so happy to have their daughter back! She wasn't the baby they'd lost any more, now she was a lovely grown-up princess.

And although Rapunzel's hair was no longer magical, she was still the most enchanting girl that Flynn had ever met.

Sleeping Beauty

Aurora and the Helpful Dragon

"I'll race you to the lookout point!" Princess Aurora called to Prince Phillip as they galloped through the forest one sunny morning. She sped away on her horse, Buttercup, with Prince Phillip close behind.

As they rounded a bend, a small dragon popped out from behind a tree.

The prince and princess went to it at once.

"*Grrgrrgrr?*" the little dragon said softly.

"Oh, he's so cute!" Aurora exclaimed.

Phillip was worried. "Dragons can be dangerous!"

The little dragon shook his head.

Aurora laughed. "I think he's saying he's not dangerous. Let's take him home. I'm going to call him Crackle!"

"He does seem like a harmless little fellow," Phillip agreed.

Aurora picked up Crackle, but Buttercup was afraid. He tossed his mane and pawed the ground. Then Crackle licked the horse's nose! Buttercup blinked with surprise and nuzzled Crackle's cheek. The little dragon giggled.

"Buttercup likes Crackle!" Aurora exclaimed.

When Phillip and Aurora rode into the courtyard, the three good fairies were hanging banners for a ball. King Stefan and his wife were coming to visit.

Flora gasped when she saw Crackle. "Dragons can be dangerous."

"Remember the last one!" Fauna added.

"Oooh, I think he's sweet," Merryweather said.

"*Grrrgrr,*" Crackle babbled.

"He seems to think you're sweet, too," Aurora told Merryweather.

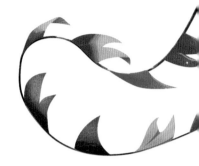

Just then, Crackle noticed a kitten in a basket of wool. Crackle listened to it purring. Then he scrunched up his mouth and closed his eyes. He tried to purr. "*Purrgrr, purrgrr!*" Clouds of smoke streamed from his nose and mouth.

"Aachoo! Aachoo! Ah-ah-ah-CHOO!" The fairies sneezed so hard from the smoke that they tumbled backwards!

Crackle looked sad for a moment. Then he saw the kitten playing with a ball of wool, and he snatched some for himself.

WHOOSH! The wool burst into flames as Crackle breathed out a small fire! Merryweather put it out with her wand.

"Oh, Crackle," Aurora said gently. "You're not a kitten. You're a dragon."

Crackle's lower lip trembled.

A moment later, Phillip led the horses into the
stable. A dog followed, barking and wagging his
tail. Crackle ran after them, wagging his tail, too.
He tried to bark. *"Woofgrr, woofgrr."*

Flames shot from his mouth and some
straw caught fire. Phillip poured water
on the burning straw.

"You're not a dog,"
he said kindly.

Sadly, the little
dragon crept out
of the stable.

Aurora noticed that Crackle looked unhappy, so she took him to the castle. As the princess began to tell a story, a bird sang by the window.

Crackle's ears perked up. He tried to sing like a bird.

"*LAAAlaagrr!*" he bellowed.

King Hubert heard the racket and rushed into the room.

"Oh, my, my, my! How did a dragon get in here?" he shouted.

Crackle had never heard a loud, angry voice before. Frightened, he ran to the garden.

Aurora chased after Crackle. At last, she found the little dragon sitting beside a fountain, watching a fish.

Splash! Before Aurora could stop him, Crackle jumped into the water.

"Crackle, you're not a fish!" Aurora exclaimed as she pulled the dragon from the pool. "You're not a kitten, or a dog, or a bird either. You're a dragon!"

Tears rolled down Crackle's face. "*Grrgrrgrr,*" he sobbed.

Suddenly, Aurora understood.

"Do you think no one will like you because you're a dragon?" she asked.

Crackle nodded and whimpered.

"You can't change what you are," Aurora said kindly. "But you don't have to be dangerous. You can be a helpful dragon."

Crackle stopped crying.

"*Grrgrrgrrgrr?*" he murmured hopefully.

Before Aurora could answer, thunder boomed and dark
clouds covered the sky. As Aurora and Crackle ran back to
the castle, rain began to pour down. Everyone was gathered
in the grand hallway, watching the storm.

"I'm afraid King Stefan and the queen might lose their way,"
Prince Phillip said, concerned.

Aurora looked at Crackle. "Do you want to show everyone
that you're a kind, brave dragon?" she asked.

"*GRRRgrrrgrr!*" Crackle exclaimed enthusiastically.

"Fly to the top of the highest tower," Aurora instructed.
"Then blow the largest, brightest flames you can to help guide
my parents to the castle."

A moment later, the little dragon soared upwards.

"Be careful!" the princess called.

Everyone tried to see Crackle, but it was too dark.

Suddenly, gold and red flames lit up the sky above the watchtower. Crackle had done it!

Again and again, Crackle blew his flames.

At last, Phillip shouted, "I see King Stefan's coach! They're almost here!"

Everyone hurried to greet the visitors.

"The tower light saved us!" King Stefan exclaimed. "I need one like it!"

At that moment Crackle flew into the hall.

"Well, there he is! Our new tower light," King Hubert said with a laugh.

"A dragon?" King Stefan asked. "But dragons are danger–"

"Not Crackle," Aurora interrupted. "He's a brave and helpful dragon!"

THE LITTLE MERMAID

Ariel to the Rescue

"Oh, Eric! This is wonderful!" Ariel smiled, as she twirled around the ballroom with her prince. "I can dance with you and see the ocean."

"Do you miss your sea friends?" he asked.

"Sometimes," Ariel replied a bit sadly. "But I love being with you."

Bright and early the next morning, Prince Eric saw Ariel walking along the beach. He caught up with her, and they strolled together along the sand. The prince knew Ariel was hoping to visit Flounder and Sebastian, as well as her other friends from the sea. But they were nowhere to be found.

Eric and Ariel watched the waves crash on to the shore.

"It's rough out there today. If I were a fish, I think I might be too scared to come close to the shore," the prince said gently. "Don't worry, Ariel. We'll figure out a way to bring together the land and the sea."

At dusk, Ariel went to Eric.

"I was thinking about what you said earlier," she said. "I want to show you something."

Ariel led the prince to the quiet lagoon they had rowed in long ago.

"Do you think my friends would feel safer visiting me here?" she asked.

Eric rubbed his chin. "*Hmmm*. Maybe."

He had an idea, but he wanted to make sure it would work before he said anything to Ariel.

A few weeks later, Eric found Ariel walking along the beach again.
"Come with me," he said. "I have a surprise for you."

He took her to the lagoon. The first thing Ariel noticed was that it
now had a big wall round it. The wall would keep out dangerous sea
creatures, such as sharks, but it also had a gate so that Ariel's friends
could enter the lagoon. In fact, Flounder, Scuttle and Sebastian were
there to greet her.

"Isn't this a great idea?" Scuttle said. "I helped, you know."

Ariel was thrilled. "Oh, Eric! I love it!"

Ariel was so excited that she waded into the water to greet her friends. Then she saw something in the lagoon.

"Look!" she exclaimed.

As they watched, a small dolphin leaped out of the water.

"He's just a baby. I wonder where his mother is," Flounder said.

He swam across the lagoon, but the baby dolphin raced away.

"Poor little guy," Flounder said. "He seems scared of me."

But Ariel wouldn't give up. Soon she had coaxed the baby to swim over to her.

"I wish there was something more we could do," Ariel said.

"I bet his mother is on the other side of that wall. Don't worry," Flounder said. "We'll find her!"

But a few days later, Sebastian and Flounder still hadn't found the dolphin's mother.

"This is terrible," Sebastian said. "We have looked everywhere under the sea, but cannot find the baby's mother. What should we do?"

Ariel looked at the little dolphin. Tomorrow she would ask more of her friends from under the sea to help.

Later that night, Ariel awoke to the sound of thunder. From the palace, she saw big waves crashing on the shore.

Eric joined her. "Are you worried about that baby dolphin?" he asked.

"He must be terrified," Ariel replied. "We need to go to him."

Eric followed Ariel into the stormy night. When they arrived at the lagoon, Flounder was trying to calm the frightened baby dolphin.

Ariel climbed on to the lagoon wall and called to the sea creatures. "Help me, please! I am Ariel, Princess of the Seas. I need my father, King Triton."

A whale was the first to respond. Then a school of fish flashed their fins.

"Thank you!" the princess shouted.

Below the surface, sea creatures raced to find King Triton.

Ariel returned to Eric.

"I know my father will be able to help," she told him.

While they waited, Eric jumped into the sea and led the dolphin to calmer waters.

Suddenly, there was a flash of light! King Triton had arrived. The storm quietened down. The baby dolphin's mother was at the lagoon gate, frantically trying to get in.

"Oh, dear!" Ariel exclaimed. "The gate won't open! She can't get in!"

Eric looked at King Triton. "Do you mind?"

"Not at all," the king replied. "Swim back, everyone!"

He raised his trident and blasted down the wall. The dolphins swam to each other, and then the baby went to Triton to thank him.

As the moon rose that night, Eric and Ariel returned to the lagoon to be with their friends.

The baby dolphin and his mother swam up and playfully splashed the prince and princess.

"I think that means we are forgiven!" Ariel said with a laugh.